T0130333

Bill Van Parys

Ricardo's Curse and others

AuthorHouse™
1663 Liberty Drive
Bloomington, IN 47403
www.authorhouse.com
Phone: 833-262-8899

This book is printed on acid-free paper.

ISBN: 978-1-6655-1090-5 (sc)
ISBN: 978-1-6655-1091-2 (e)

Print information available on the last page.

Published by AuthorHouse 12/11/2020

authorHOUSE®

Ricardo's Curse and others

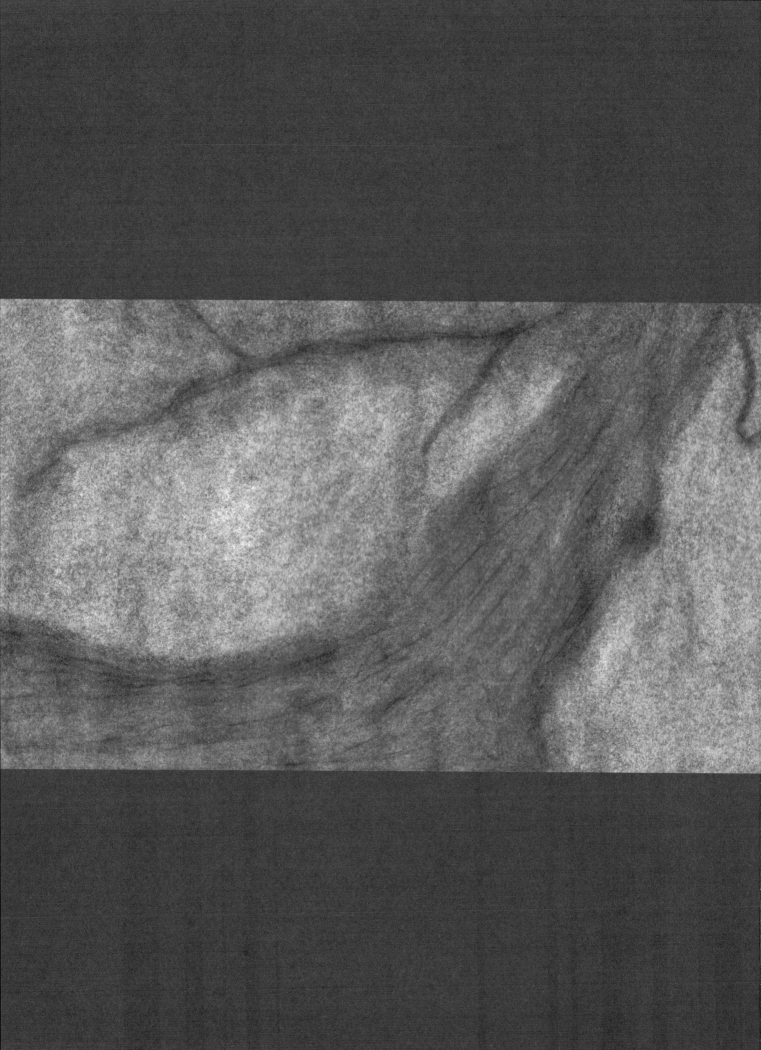

Contents

Ricardo's Curse

1: My name is Ricardo Montoya, I like to have sexual relations with the dead. That is to say, I like to fuck corpses!!! Heh heh heh heh!

One night as I was working late, the body of a woman I had a crush on in high school, was wheeled in for my usual postmortem preparatory work.

I couldn't help remembering the party where we were both in attendance, when I asked her out. Being very drunk, her response was immediate and unsavory. She vomited all over my penny-loafers! I was crestfallen, and I never completely recovered from the experience. To calm my nerves, I went home and masturbated to her yearbook photo!

I was a pathetic fool in my school days, I know. But I am much better now, I can assure you.

As Tony, one of the orderlies brought in the body, we exchanged jokes and pleasantries, and with that, he left and I was alone with the body. I quickly locked the door. With my pants and lab coat removed, I climbed onto the gurney very carefully and slid my semi-erect penis into her slack and lifeless vagina.

2: I got a violent start, and nearly shit all over the place! When I looked at Ellie's face and discovered that her eyes were open. It startled me because, her eyes had been closed when she was wheeled in.

I had to get off of her and recompose myself. My heart felt as if it might just rip its way out of my chest.

In a cabinet in the corner, was a bottle of "medicinal" brandy, I took a long swallow and went back to my "work".

As I was recapping the bottle, I heard a sigh from the other side of the room. I very nearly dropped the bottle! With shaky hands I returned the bottle to the shelf.

I decided to give Eleanor another go. I taped her eyes shut, so I would not have to look into her lifeless eyes, as I did the deed.

As I was building up a rhythm, Ellie's eyes suddenly popped open, in spite of the masking tape! I cried out in horror, but before I could react, she reached over with her left hand and grabbed my rapidly deflating member! In a blind panic, I leaned back on my knees in a futile attempt at escape. Eleanor, held firm in a death grip (pun intended), and I pulled her up into a sitting position in front of me.

3: Eleanor's mouth opened mechanically in an apparent attempt to kiss me. Crying out with revulsion, I pitched backward off of the table, taking Ellie with me.

On the floor we tussled, I tried to fight her off, but couldn't. Straddling me, she leaned down to me. It seemed she did want to kiss me after all!

Rather than kiss me, her mouth opened mechanically, and this time dirty water from the lake she'd drowned in, spewed from her, covering my face and head in leaves and other detritus from the lake.

I screamed until it felt as if my lungs would burst!

I came to fully clothed, my face and hair were dry. Across the room, Eleanor lay still on the examination table where she had been since Tony had wheeled her in. The back of my head hurt. Evidently, I had fallen, hit my head hard enough to knock myself out, and dreamt the entire ordeal with Eleanor.

The back of my head was bleeding slightly. No big deal, although I would have a hellacious headache later most likely.

I rubbed the back of my head, realizing I had hurt it more than I originally believed. I may have even had a concussion.

4: While massaging my head, I discovered that my hair was somewhat damp and there was some grit on my scalp. Odd, considering it was all a nightmare, brought on by my head trauma!

Stuck in the collar of my lab coat, were leaves, more grit and a few twigs. I took off the coat, and noted that it was wet and sandy and there appeared, more leaves and twigs.

It had all happened! Every bit of my struggle with Eleanor had occurred!

I asked Tony, to call in another mortician to take over for me. I suddenly took ill I explained, and needed to leave immediately.

When I got home, I showered. In my robe, I sat at my computer, and updated my resume'. Then I typed out my letter of resignation.

My superiors were shocked! Mrs. Hutchison said it best; 'You were always so deeply into your work', (she had no idea how right she was!!! Hee hee hee!).

I then got into a much safer line of work.

Thus is the story of how I, Ricardo Montoya, became one of the best real estate agents in the Southeast. HALLELUJAH!!!

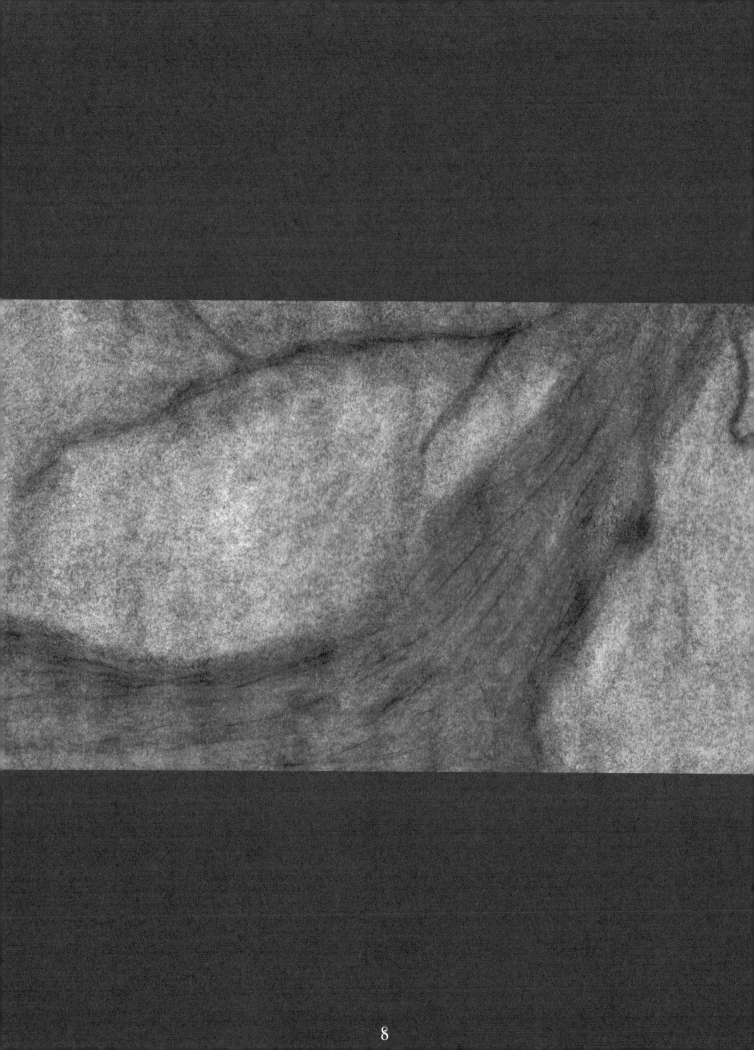

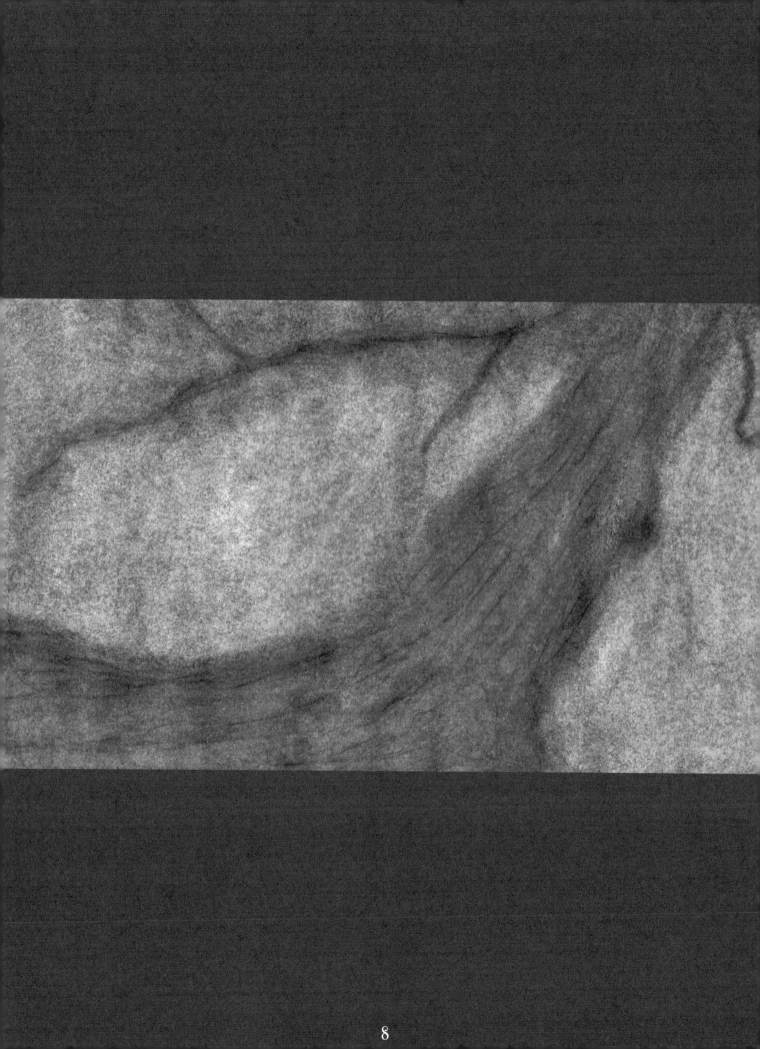

A SNIPER'S TALE
(THE DEAD WIFE'S WARNING)

part 1

The dreams had been getting progressively worse. Jake Tupelo's dead wife Wilma, had beckoned to him from across a bottomless chasm. She was warning him not to look into the pit. Lest he might learn something damaging to his psyche.

From across the chasm, Wilma did not appear to Jake in any real detail, she seemed to be nothing more than a slightly misshapen outline. A sort of ghostly image.

Since that first dream of Wilma, she had appeared to him in horrific detail. Looking not like she had in life, but rather as she would be after two years in her grave. The horror and revulsion he felt initially, was indescribable. He had since hardened to her appearance and had forced himself to learn the meaning of her sudden apparition two years after her death.

part 2

Jake Tupelo, had been so distraught by Wilma's death, that he had attempted suicide on three separate occasions. Wilma's illness, had taken an enormous toll on Jake's emotional and physical well being. For nearly ten years, Wilma had endured chemotherapy and radiation treatments, even experimental drugs.

She had also tried Hoodoo! All to no avail.

To Wilma, it became obvious that she was dying. Jake, had maintained hope that Wilma would survive. Jake's, first attempt at suicide, came just three weeks after Wilma's funeral.

part 3

In his recurrent nightmare, Jake couldn't discern Wilma's message. He couldn't understand if he was intended to look into the abyss, or if he should avoid looking.

It always began the same way. Jake found himself wandering through a bleak landscape, the predominant colors were blacks and greys. Any vegetation appeared not merely dead, but dried out. He would walk on until he came near to a jagged mountain range. At first appearance, what stopped him appeared to be a lake. Upon closer inspection, what appeared was an enormous hole in the ground. Standing on the other side of the abyss, was his dead wife Wilma. She was waving to Jake from the other side, frantically trying to warn him to some onrushing danger.

Over the next few months, the dreams became more insistent. Jake even had them by day!

In addition to the dreams, during his waking hours, Jake would see fleeting shadows, dart about from room to room. One of these, took on a slumped, but somehow familiar form.

At precisely 3:15 A.M. one morning, Jake Tupelo, was frightened awake by an unearthly shrieking. He fell out of bed and hit his head on the end table next to his bed.

A few days later, Jake noted a stench that combined that of rotten meat, mold and mildew, wet earth and rotted plant matter. It was such an overpowering odor, that it caused him to wretch, and nearly vomit on the floor.

Over the next weeks, Jake began to find muddy footprints that issued from nowhere and stopped by his bed.

part 4

Six months into the paranormal activity, Jake was startled awake by the unearthly shrieking he had heard months before.

When he opened his eyes and looked around, Jake gave voice to a full-throated shriek of his own. Wilma, was standing slump-shouldered next to his bed!

Wilma, appeared the way he imagined she would look after two years in her grave. Grave beetles wriggling through her hair (one of them crawled out of her mouth and made its way down into her shriveled cleavage), a few maggots and larger grave worms, moving around on her.

Both of her eyes were missing, yet she seemed to be looking at him

It slowly dawned on Jake, that he might be dreaming. But this was unlike any dream he had had to date. Jake was reasonably sure that he could not smell anything in a dream. Yet he smelled an overwhelming stench of death.

This was the beginning of the ritual that would culminate with Jacob Eugene Tupelo III, climbing up into the belfry of a local church, shooting at and killing a large number of people on the surrounding grounds.

part 5

At a small church in Newton, North Carolina, Jake Tupelo, walked boldly in with a hunting rifle slung over his shoulder, and a nine millimeter Glock handgun, on his left hip in a holster turned backward so it could be drawn with either hand.

Jake seized the first clergyman he encountered, drew the gun with his left hand, and ordered the other clergymen to chew the floor.

With his new hostage, they slowly made their way to the tower door. It was locked.

Jake ordered the key holder to come forward, unlock the door, and get the hell out of the way!

With the door unlocked, Jake and the clergyman, carefully moved up the stairs.

The whole way, Jake was yelling at Wilma to leave well enough alone and stay out of his way.

The clergyman, hadn't the slightest idea to whom Jake was yelling, so he kept quiet. In his estimation, the madman did not need any more reasons to kill him.

Halfway up the stairs Jake stopped, and yelled for the key holder once again. When the man stepped into view (cautiously), Jake ordered the man to track down some lumber, nails and a hammer. After a brief plea for the madman to take him instead (and was vehemently turned down), the key holder complied.

Hammer and nails were not a problem, however, the wood the gunman required, was more problematic. This was solved, when the neighbor of one of the parishioners had some old two-by-fours lying around his backyard.

The wood was quickly taken to the church on a flat-bed trailer pulled by the man's riding lawn mower.

After turning loose the two clergymen, Jake Tupelo, built himself a barricade in the belfry tower. From there, he could shoot whomever he wished.

part 6

Over the next few weeks, Wilma tried to make Jake understand her message. She made clear that her message was a desperate one, and that he needed to understand her. That much was clear enough to Jake.

With the alphabet refrigerator magnets, Wilma, would spell out words; JAKE, WILMA, TOWER, GUN, DON'T, and KILL. This evidently, was a means of communication that she could not use regularly.

Wilma, made clear that Jake, was on a crash-course with a very negative venture, but she could not properly articulate her message.

One morning, the refrigerator magnets spelled out, CHURCH! Jake, took this to mean that he should attend church. Later that evening, the word STUPID, was spelled out.

On another occasion, the words, DON'T CHURCH, was spelled out.

part 7

After the barricade was completed, Jake set up his sniper's nest. That done, he pistol-whipped the clergyman (who had stayed too close at hand!), then bound and gagged him, and placed him inside the building out of harm's way.

Jake, got behind the barricade, and took aim. He chose lunchtime as his starting time. Within a minute or so, he had a target.

All the while, he continued to argue with Wilma. He would not be deterred from his course of action, no matter how violently she argued with Jake.

part 8

Wilma, rushed at Jake just as he took the first shot, but he hit his target anyway. Another parishioner who happened to be walking away from the church just as Jake Tupelo, took his first shot, was the first victim. The right side of his head, disappeared into a red mist. A woman walking toward the church, promptly vomited, just before she too was felled by Jake's second shot. The bullet caught her in the throat, killing her almost instantly.

part 9

Shortly before writing his final memoir, Jake had another dream that he had nearly as often as his "prophetic" dream. This one, a throwback to a time when Wilma was going through her chemo and radiation treatments. She was nearly always sick and in pain. He had often thought that he should just shoot her and put her out of her misery, but in the end, he was too cowardly. Wilma, simply wasted away.

Jake, had started awake with the realization that he had once again wet the bed. He didn't care anymore.

part 10

After killing the puking woman people began screaming and looking about frantically for the sniper. No one knew that he was in the belfry tower of the nearby church.

Although he was never in the military, Jake Tupelo had been a crack shot due to his many hunting trips. Jake, had become adept at hitting his targets exactly where he wanted to that is why he was up to this particular challenge.

part 11

As people were running this way and that, Jake continued to pick off his targets with reckless abandon.

One by one, citizens and law enforcement officers, fired back from cover. They hid behind cars, low brick walls, from around buildings, even trees too narrow to hide behind, but no one could hit the "Belfry Sniper."

part 12

Like a "will-o-the-wisp" in the night, she came to him. Convincing him to reconsider his course of action and surrender before things got any worse was simply impossible.

part 13

It must have been some imp of the perverse, but one of the altar boys decided to test the durability of the tower sniper's barricade. What he discovered, was the door was secured from the wrong side.

The barricade, allowed for the door to be opened from inside the building. The "Belfry Sniper", was vulnerable to attack from within, without his knowledge.

The altar boy, freed the clergyman, who in turn waited for the police to arrive.

part 14

Just that morning, Jake completed his suicide note, grabbed his guns, and set out for his date with infamy. Wilma, could not decide whether Jake was ignoring her, or if he could no longer see her. But try as she might, he completely ignored her, or simply didn't see her.

In the nightmare, Jake finally peered into the abyss, and saw himself in the belfry tower of a local church taking aim on the unwary passersby. He smiled at the realization that he had gained a new lease on life, taking charge after a lifetime of not knowing his place in the world at large. He finally had a purpose! Albeit an infamous one.

In the nightmare, Wilma screamed, and vanished, leaving Jake to wander the bleak landscape all alone. He chose to jump into the abyss, and face his destiny head-on.

Sometimes, he dreamt of wrecking balls, crashing through the walls of his house, trying to kill him. He had visions when he was awake. One of which, saw his electric razor, coming to life in his hand, trying to attack him!

Often, everyday chores, would become an ordeal. Since Wilma's death, the house began to crumble around Jake. Paint began to peel, toilets would plug up or simply not work. One day as he opened a window, the whole window (frame and all), fell out and shattered. Doorknobs, pulled off in his hand. You name it! It broke!

part 16

A virtual militia, was beginning to form out of sight of the church tower. They brought hunting rifles (like the one that Jake Tupelo, was using), shotguns (just in case they got in close), pistols (no good for distant targets), slingshots, and BB guns, among others. They hoped to get in close, so aiming was not such a problem.

The body count continued to rise. Jake, had now killed thirteen, and wounded ten. Twenty-three lives, forever changed in an instant of lead and gunpowder. Not to mention their friends and families lives.

part 17

The police, were assembling outside of the church, asking militiamen and even women, to hold back and let them handle the madman. A fight ensued, two militiamen were killed, one injured, also one police officer was seriously wounded.

As the police/militia battle was taking place, the "Belfry Sniper", was firing in rapid succession, not hitting anyone, but keeping everyone on their toes just the same.

part 18

An errant shot, took off most of his right ear, causing him to drop his .30-.30 hunting rifle. The rifle discharged harmlessly when it landed at the bottom of the tower.

Jake Tupelo, sat back and waited for the inevitable showdown. He would go out in a blaze of glory. Failing that, he would save one last shot for himself.

Wilma, appeared to him for the last time.

"Why did you do this Jake?" she asked him.

"I can't live without you Wilma, I just can't do it." He responded.

And then he added "I'm sorry."

part 19

Downstairs, the assembled police officers, charged up the stairwell to the top of the belfry tower, in the hope of taking the belfry sniper by surprise. They had no way of knowing that the madman had capitulated. There would be more gunfire and death before this little "shadow play", had played out.

part 20

The altar boy, threw the door open wide, startling the gunman. Jake Tupelo's, reaction was instantaneous, he shot the boy in the right leg, and the boy collapsed to the floor, howling in pain.

Seconds later, Jake and the police, were exchanging gunfire right over the terrified and injured altar boy. He peed his pants during the exchange! So did one of the injured officers, who had been shot in the chest.

One of the officers, using his pump-action shotgun, pumped two rounds directly into the face of Jacob Eugene Tupelo III, killing him instantly.

part 21

In the aftermath, two officers died in the taking of the belfry tower. The "Belfry Sniper", and two officers, were the only fatalities within the church itself. Incredible, considering the "firefight" within.

part 22

Wilma Tupelo, shook her head sadly, went back to the cemetery, and walked into her grave as if she were descending a flight of stairs. No one but Jake, ever saw her. The question is, was she real, or just a figment of Jake's diseased imagination?

THE END ? ? ?

DRACULA SUCKS!!!

Setting: A young woman's bedroom in the dead of night.

A large vampire-bat, alights outside the window visible through the sheer white curtains of a young woman's bedroom. With a puff of smoke, the bat becomes Dracula. With one arm, he conceals his face with his cape as he silently creeps across the room. Quietly leaning over the sleeping woman, he silently places his false teeth (complete with hollow fangs!!!), into his mouth and prepares to dine.

The woman awakens, and a terrified expression crosses her face, briefly. She then says; "I'm sorry you wasted your time coming here, but I'm anemic"!

With a sigh, he shrugs, removes his false teeth (complete with hollow fangs!!!) from his mouth, puts them back into their ornate case, and retraces his steps.

Outside he muses to himself; "this has been a dreadful night, I wish I had tried the next town over instead". Just how many people are anemic these days anyway?! It seems as if people are either anemic or donating blood these days. Just what is the "King of Vampires" to do to get a nice hot meal?!

And that was the story of how Vlad Dracula, came to work as a butcher.

Jack O' Lantern, and the House of Vanishing Points

Jack O' Lantern, it is you who sits upon your pedestal,
Out in front of the house of vanishing points!
Vanishing points to nowhere they will go,
Whence winds can never blow.
From your pedestal, you cannot traverse,
You will be kept from that infinite universe.
To a land of always night,
To be removed from your blight.
But it is not to be so,
To a garbage dump you will go.
Jack O' Lantern, and the house of vanishing points,
Are caught in space,
To be captured forever in deadly embrace!!!

MIDNIGHT IN THE WELL OF SOULS

Midnight in the well of souls.
Halloween is great,
Candy by the handfuls, I ate.
Evil ghosts come out of their holes,
Some ghosts are good, some are bad,
And some are totally rad!!!
Halloween Rocks!!!
It makes me want to put on my socks.
The moon's ghostly pallor,
Fills me with valor.
Darkness comes, and darkness falls,
Too much candy, sends me bouncing from the walls,
And down the halls!!!
Midnight in the well of souls.

Mr. Pumpkin, The Diabolical

O' Mr. Pumpkin the diabolical one!!!
Your eyes so yellow,
Are the yellowest of yellow.
As the kiddies prance in their fright masks,
You look on in your infinite dispassion.
But they don't know your secret,
Since you haven't a mouth, how will you divulge your secret?
O' Mr. Pumpkin the diabolical one,
After Halloween you will sleep the sleep of the damn'd

Odd House of Bad Angles

The odd house of bad angles, you look so chipper,
One day you will go to the wood chipper.
To be torn asunder,
In your infinite blunder.
Imperfect is your thatch,
Your walls, doors, and windows, do not match!
Your usage of colors suck,
For you, I do not give a buck!!!
Everything about you is wrong,
To the market you will go for a song.
Odd house of bad angles,
Oh you of your obtuse angles!!!

SUMMER RAINS

SUMMER RAINS
SOMETIMES THEY FALL HEAVY
SOMETIMES THEY FALL STEADY
SOMETIMES THEY BRING FIREFLIES
SOMETIMES THEY BRING DANDELIONS.
SOMETIMES THEY FALL IN TIME
SUMMER RAINS
SOMETIMES THEY BRING GLOOM AND DOOM
SOMETIMES THEY MAKE THINGS BLOOM
SUMMER RAINS SOMETIMES COME NEAR
SUMMER RAINS COME EVERY YEAR...

SUMMER SOLSTICE

JULY IS VERY HOT
NATURE BATHED IN SUMMER
MY HEART LIES THERE TOO...

THE DARKSTALKER COMETH

He who stalketh the night,
Who bringeth the blight.
Cometh within sight,
To bringeth on the light.
He who stalketh the night.

He who stalketh the night,
Who bringeth the blight.
Cometh within sight,
To bringeth the light.
He who stalketh the night.

The MOON Frowns on SILVERY BLIGHT

I am the Moon who frowns on Silvery Blight!!!
Blight of Silver, forsaken by the Moon.
The Moon, shines brightly upon Silvery Blight.
Silvery Blight, is brightly lit by the Moon.
Silvery Blight and the Moon, are forsaken by the Night.
The Night forsakes the Moon, but fears Silvery Blight.
The Moon and the Night, fear Silvery Blight.

UNWANTED TELEPHONE CALL RESPONSES

"Van Parys Mortuary, where you":

1: Kill'em we grill'em

2: Still'em we chill'em

3: Stab'em we slab'em

4: Gash'em we ash'em

5: Slay'em we fillet'em

6: Lay'em we fillet'em

7: Blast'em we gassed'em

8: Bump'em off we dump'em off

9: Whack'em we stack'em

10: Waste'em we taste'em

11: Gas'em we pass'em

12: Zip'em we unzip'em

13: Fillet'em we sauttee'em

14: Slash'em we stash'em

15: Blast'em we cast'em

16: Run'em over we cover'em over

17: Skewer'em we pewter'em

18: Gones'em we bronze'em

19: Gash'em we stash'em

20: Rip'em we zip'em

21: Lay'em we sauttee'em

Printed in the United States
By Bookmasters